JPIC Gee
Gee, Kimberly
Today with Meg and Ted

$12.99
ocn609529826
01/05/2011

S0-AEP-604

For Finn and Claire, my real-life inspirations

Published in the United States by Golden Books, an imprint of Random House Children's Books,
a division of Random House, Inc., 1745 Broadway, New York, NY 10019. Golden Books, A Golden Book,
and the G colophon are registered trademarks of Random House, Inc.
www.randomhouse.com/kids
Educators and librarians, for a variety of teaching tools, visit us at www.randomhouse.com/teachers
Library of Congress Control Number: 2009936944
ISBN: 978-0-375-86717-0 (trade)—ISBN: 978-0-375-96717-7 (lib. bdg.)
PRINTED IN CHINA
10 9 8 7 6 5 4 3 2 1

Random House Children's Books supports the First Amendment and celebrates the right to read.

Today

with Meg and Ted

By Kimberly Gee

🌼 A GOLDEN BOOK · NEW YORK

Today is a good day.

Today is a good day to hold on tight.

Today is a good
day to just let go!

Today is a good day
to be very still.

Today is a good day to be very, very quick!

Today is a good day to ask for help.

Today is a good day
to give help, too.

Today is a good day
to stand on one foot.

And today is a good day to look at a foot.

Today is a good day to look at things in a new way.

And today is a good day to stick with what we know.

It is always a good
day for lunch!

Today is a good day
to be ourselves.

Today is a good day
to be wild gorillas!

Today is a good day for some quiet time, alone.

Today is a good day to eat our favorite food . . .

and to try something new.

Today is a good day for a sticky mess.

Today is a good day
to be squeaky-clean.

Today is a good day to be freeee!

Today is a good day to be close and cozy.

And today is a good day
to dream about tomorrow.